Text © 2014 by M.R. Nelson
Illustration © 2014 by Holly Liminton

All rights reserved
No portion of this book may be reproduced without express permission of the publisher
First Edition
ARC ISBN: 978-1500112660
Hardcover ISBN: 978-1-62395-590-8

Published in the United States by Xist Publishing
PO Box 61593
Irvine CA 92602
www.xistpublishing.com

Petunia, The Girl Who Was NOT a Princess

Once upon a time, there was a little girl named Petunia. Petunia didn't live in a castle, and she was NOT a princess!

Well, sometimes she pretended her house was a castle, but she was most definitely NOT a princess!

Most of the girls Petunia knew liked to be princesses. They dressed in frilly dresses and held pretend balls with pretend princes.

Petunia preferred to wear her favorite old sweatshirt (the one with the frog on the front).

She liked to run around in the field by her house and play ball.

She liked to catch lizards and climb trees.

She liked to build towers and race cars.

But she was lonely.
She wished she had a friend who would run and play, build and race, catch and climb, and stomp and make mud pies with her.

So Petunia was very excited when a new family moved into the castle up the street.

She was even more excited when her parents told her the new family had a little girl named Penelope, who was about the same age as Petunia.

But she was NOT excited when she first saw Penelope. Penelope wore a flouncy pink and purple dress with bows and sparkles and she had a crown on her head.

"Oh no not another PRINCESS!" thought Petunia.

A little while later, she heard someone else clambering up the tree. She looked down and saw that it was Penelope.

"Do you want to play ball with me?"

Penelope asked.

She could build enormous towers

And next time it rained, Penelope showed Petunia her secret royal recipe for mud cakes, which were even better than mud pies.

Some of the other princesses discovered they liked some of the same things Petunia did, too. There were even enough princesses who liked to play ball to have a proper soccer game.

Petunia and Penelope became best friends. They defended their castles from wild trolls wielding battering rams...

And charmed the King of the Forest Lands into joining them for tea.

They tamed
fierce dragons...

And tricked the Fairy Queen into giving them double the usual reward.

Penelope even convinced Petunia to wear a moderately frilly dress and go to a pretend ball with other princesses and their princes.

Petunia still preferred her favourite sweatshirt with the frog on the front, but she discovered that she liked to dance - with or without a prince.

And she lived happily ever after.

CPSIA information can be obtained
at www.ICGtesting.com
Printed in the USA
LVIC05n0214081214
417725LV00012B/23